This book is dedicated to Isaac Parsons.

Thanks to Ash and Joey for Meesha's paintings.

BLOOMSBURY CHILDREN'S BOOKS
Bloomsbury Publishing Inc., part of Bloomsbury Publishing Plc
1385 Broadway, New York, NY 10018

BLOOMSBURY, BLOOMSBURY CHILDREN'S BOOKS, and the Diana logo
are trademarks of Bloomsbury Publishing Plc

First published in Great Britain in July 2020 by Bloomsbury Publishing Plc
Published in the United States of America in February 2021
by Bloomsbury Children's Books

Bloomsbury books may be purchased for business or promotional use. For information on bulk purchases please contact
Macmillan Corporate and Premium Sales Department at specialmarkets@macmillan.com

Library of Congress Cataloging-in-Publication Data
available upon request
LCCN: 2020024579
ISBN 978-1-5476-0519-4 (hardcover)
ISBN 978-1-5476-0520-0 (e-book) • ISBN 978-1-5476-0521-7 (e-PDF)

Art created digitally on an iPad Pro with a selection of natural media brushes in Procreate
Typeset in Appareo Medium • Book design by Goldy Broad
Printed and bound in China by Leo Paper Products, Heshan, Guangdong
4 6 8 10 9 7 5 3

To find out more about our authors and books visit www.bloomsbury.com and sign up for our newsletters.

MEESHA
MAKES FRIENDS

TOM PERCIVAL

BLOOMSBURY
CHILDREN'S BOOKS
NEW YORK LONDON OXFORD NEW DELHI SYDNEY

Meesha LOVED
making things.

She could make pictures
out of numbers . . .

and pictures
out of sounds.

Sometimes she made
pictures out of *both*.

But there was one thing that Meesha
found hard to make . . .

friends.

Everybody else seemed to find it easy. But not Meesha.

When she tried, she didn't know what to do, what to say, or *when* to say it.

For Meesha, making friends was so difficult
that she wondered if she would *ever*
be able to do it.

Then, one evening, Meesha had an idea.
She got out her paints, her pencils,
and all her other tools.

Then she started to
cut and stick and
glue and sew.

Soon she had made a
whole *group* of really fun friends.

Friends that were easy
to be around.

Friends that she could take with her
wherever she went.

Admittedly, Meesha's new friends weren't very good at tennis . . .

or soccer . . .

or catch.

But Meesha felt comfortable with them,
and *that* was what mattered.

One day, Meesha's
mom said they were
going to a party.

She *said* there
would be lots of
nice people there.

She *said* it would be fun.

Meesha wasn't so sure.

The party was noisy, chaotic, and unpredictable.
Everyone else was playing together . . .

and Meesha just *couldn't*
find a way to join in.

She ran off to find a quiet corner
where she could make her *own* friends.

Meesha sat happily for a while until
she realized that something didn't feel right.

A boy was watching her.

He said, "Hi, I'm Josh.
Can I see what you're
making?"

For a while Meesha said nothing.

But then she took a deep breath
and showed him her friends.

"Wow!" gasped Josh. "They're amazing!
Can you show me how to make one?"

Meesha was worried.

What if he got it all wrong?
What if he ruined everything?

But Josh didn't *look* like he would
try to ruin things. So . . .

. . . Meesha showed him what to do.

And do you know what? Josh *didn't* get it all wrong, and he didn't ruin anything either.

In fact, now that she was making things
with someone else . . .

it was *even* better!

Soon Meesha *and* Josh had built
a whole town for their friends
to live in—*together*.

"Let's go and show the others!" said Josh.

Meesha wasn't sure.

But Josh's smile made her feel that
it would all be okay.

AND IT WAS!

For the first time *ever* Meesha knew
exactly what to say *and* what to do.

And that was how the friends
that Meesha made . . .

. . . helped Meesha make friends.

Dear Reader,

This is a book about a girl who finds it hard to make friends.

Making friends is one of those things that *looks* really easy, but it can sometimes feel like the hardest thing in the world!

If you ever find it hard to make friends, then a great place to start is speaking to children who seem to enjoy the same things as you, whether that's music, art, soccer, rock climbing, ice skating, or ANYTHING at all!

And if you ever see someone who looks a little bit "on-their-own"— try to include them. Ask them what they like to do. You never know, it might be something that YOU love to do as well, and you might have just met your new best friend!

No matter what you're feeling, remember that it always helps to talk about it. Be open, be honest, be YOU!

Love,

TOM

Here's an organization that offers resources if you're interested in learning more: **childmind.org**